# Victor and Hugo

ROBERT J. BLAKE

Philomel Books

The city of Paris was waking up.
Pierre the baker was handing out goodies.
Grumpy Max was warming up his pipe organ.
And Maestro was stacking colorful boxes on the bridge.
"Ahhh-ha-ha!" said a group watching Victor wave from his basket.
"Oooh...whoa!" said the crowd watching Hugo balance on the boxes.
"What now?" people wondered when Maestro moved his hands away from the accordion.

"*Vrr-trr!*" Victor barked two barks.

*Vrr-trr!* The accordion answered all on its own.

"*Hrr-roo!*" Hugo barked.

*Hrr-roo!* The accordion matched him exactly.

"*Mrr-tro!*" Maestro called.

*Mrr-tro!* The accordion sounded.

"Surely there is magic in that accordion!" a woman said.

"Hmph!" said Grumpy Max.

Maestro put his hands
to the accordion and played
his new song called "Magic in Paris."
    Hugo sang while standing on the boxes.
Victor sang while doing backflips.
    The crowd danced and threw coins.
    When the song ended, a man with a violin asked, "Maestro,
may we musicians join in your magic?"
    Maestro smiled. "Let us all sing and dance and play!"
    And so everyone sang, everyone danced, and every musician played—
except Grumpy Max, the organ grinder. "Bah!" He sounded a sour note.
"Magic! There is no magic in the world anymore!"
    And he tossed a salami to get the dogs to stop singing.

Victor and Hugo jumped for the salami.
"Don't eat that!" Maestro tried to stop his dogs.
"Salami will upset your voice!"
All three friends hit the railing at the same time.
Maestro and the salami fell to the bridge deck.
The accordion and Victor and Hugo fell over the side of the bridge.
And suddenly, all music everywhere stopped.

Now the only sound at all came from the
engine of a junk barge.
Then . . .
*Oof!* Victor landed on an old mattress.
*Thud!* Hugo landed on a pile of
overstuffed sacks.

Maestro called from the bridge,
"Victor! Hugo! Get the accordion!"

The accordion! Victor and Hugo scrambled over bent toys and broken ladders. They soon found it—inside an old tire!

They pulled and tugged, but the accordion would not come out.

"Oooo," Hugo cried. "It is part of the tire now—it is an accordion tire. How can Maestro play an accordion tire?"

The accordion made some feeble sounds: *Vrr-trr! Hoo-roo!* But when it tried to play two other notes, the sound faded. *Mrrrr-tro . . .*

The barge slowed down.

Then the barge stopped. A huge claw dropped out
of the sky and came right at Victor and Hugo. The dogs
jumped away as it picked up an old chair, a broken
ladder, and—oh no—the accordion tire.
The claw creaked and screamed its way over
to a waiting dump bin. But just as it opened, the
accordion tire twisted free.
It bounced onto the road and rolled away.
The dogs leaped off the barge and
chased after it.

Victor and Hugo chased the
accordion tire along the cobblestone
quay all the way back to the bridge.
"Look!" The violin player pointed.
"It's Maestro's accordion!"

Trinket sellers put down
their trinkets. Artists dropped
their brushes. Tourists even
put away their cameras!
Soon the bridge was empty
because everyone was chasing
after the accordion, yelling,
"We must have our music back!"

The accordion rolled over a sunbather and
through a flower cart.

Police blew their whistles and called out,
"STOP!"

But the accordion tire did not stop. It raced
up a street ramp, rumbled across a wooden
footbridge, and turned out onto the sidewalk.

A group of important people from the BigCity Smartguys Company came up with a plan to get the accordion—and the world's music—back. They formed a circle on the sidewalk.

"Leave one side open," the Chief Excellent Officer said.

When the accordion rolled into the circle, the workers closed in behind it.

"Got it!" the Chief said.

But they didn't.

The accordion hopped up on the stone wall and jumped over the side. Then it disappeared.

Everyone looked up, down, and all around, but no one could figure out where the accordion tire went.

But Hugo could. He put his nose to the ground and sniffed. "Hmmm. The accordion tire landed here," *SNIFF*, "and went along there and," *SNIFF* . . . He stopped at the stone wall, puzzled.

"Listen," Victor said. A small sound came from behind the wall. *Vrr-trr! Hoo-roo!*

Victor copied the sound exactly. *"Vrr-trr!"*

Hugo matched the notes exactly. *"Hoo-roo!"*

And when Victor and Hugo sounded each note, a hidden door opened just enough to let the dogs squeeze through.

Inside, the hum of machines made it impossible to hear anything else. So the dogs used their noses to follow the accordion's scent down and down. But soon a much stronger odor made it impossible to smell the accordion.

"Peeyew!" Victor said. "We are in the sewers! Now we can't hear or smell the accordion."

"It sure is wet." Hugo looked down at his paws.

Victor also looked down. And right under his paws, he saw a tire track!

He followed the marks down some stairs, across a metal girder, and around a cement wall.

"Hugo, look!"

The accordion had wedged itself between some pipes. It still played the two double notes: *Vrr-trr! Hoo-roo!* But every time it tried to play a third sound, the sound faded. *Mrrr . . .*

Victor tugged at the shoulder strap.

"The accordion is still stuck in the tire," Victor said.

"Ooo," Hugo answered.

"And I think we might be lost down here," Victor said.

"Oooooo," Hugo moaned.

"And we may never see Maestro again!"

Now they both howled, "Ooooo-ooooo!"

They howled high and howled low. Their voices echoed off the walls and vibrated the pipes.

"Oooooo-oooooo!" Victor and Hugo's unhappy notes traveled through vents and into subway tunnels. Trains stood still at the stations.

"Oooooo-oooooo!" The notes carried up the stairs, out of drains, and into the city. Cats cried and flowers drooped.

"Oooooo-oooooo!" The dogs' sad song moved along the streets, up the sides of buildings, into people's homes, and out through their chimney pots. Cars wouldn't start, doors wouldn't open, and people wouldn't eat croissants.

Soon everyone in Paris heard the sad, sad song, including the most important person of all—

Maestro!

He followed their song and came splashing through a tunnel.

"Victor! Hugo! You have found the accordion, but you made all of Paris sad with your song!"

He held his dogs close until Hugo tugged on the tire. The accordion still wouldn't budge.

"That is because some of the magic was missing!" Maestro said. "Watch and listen."

He leaned over and touched two keys. *Vrr-trr!*

"*Vrr-trr* is for Victor!" he said.

He touched two more keys. *Hoo-roo!*

"*Hoo-roo* is for Hugo!"

He touched the keys a third time and the accordion
played the missing notes, *Mrr-tro!*
"*Mrr-tro* is for Maestro!"
The accordion jumped out of the tire and
into his hands.

Maestro led the way onto the subway
platforms and out of the darkness.
"*Vrr-trr!*" sang Victor.
"*Hoo-roo!*" sang Hugo.
"*Mrr-tro!*" sang Maestro.
*Vrr-trr! Hoo-roo! Mrr-tro!* sang
the accordion.
Their happy song rose up and over
the sad sounds of the city.

On the street, a woman called out, "Surely there is magic in that accordion!"

"Ah, no!" Maestro said. "The magic is in the music."

"And the music is everywhere!" said Victor.

"But sometimes you have to go and get it back!" said Hugo.

Every person in the city danced and sang, and was happy once again. Even Grumpy Max.

## TO MY FRIEND
### DOUG CUSHMAN

I'd like to thank the BigCity Smartguys:
Ed, Jim, Mike, and Robert. Also thanks to
Luke and Gwen, Oliver, Maria, Sylvain,
Michel, Dominique, Jim Wolf, Jeff Lisenby,
and Malcolm Glass. Maestros all!

### AUTHOR'S NOTE
When you walk along the River Seine
in Paris, it seems you always experience
two things—the sound of music and
the sight of dogs playing. The beautiful
sounds make the city vibrant and alive.
The music seems to make the dogs
dance and play. And I wondered: What
would the world be like if all the music
went away? What if two dogs went to
find the music? Could they bring joy
back to the city again?

**PHILOMEL BOOKS**
an imprint of Penguin Random House LLC
375 Hudson Street, New York, NY 10014

Library of Congress Cataloging-in-
Publication Data. Blake, Robert J., author,
illustrator. Victor and Hugo / Robert J. Blake.
pages cm. Summary: When Maestro's
accordion gets stuck in a tire and then rolls
into the sewers of Paris, two dogs give chase.
[1. Dogs—Fiction. 2. Accordion—Fiction.
3. Paris (France)—Fiction. 4. France—Fiction.]
I. Title. PZ7.B564Vi 2016 [E]—dc23
2015012243. Manufactured in China by RR
Donnelley Asia Printing Solutions Ltd.
ISBN 978-0-399-24324-0
10 9 8 7 6 5 4 3 2 1

Edited by Jill Santopolo.
Design by Jennifer Chung.
Text set in 14-point Veronika LT Std.
The art for this book was done with
oil paint on canvas.

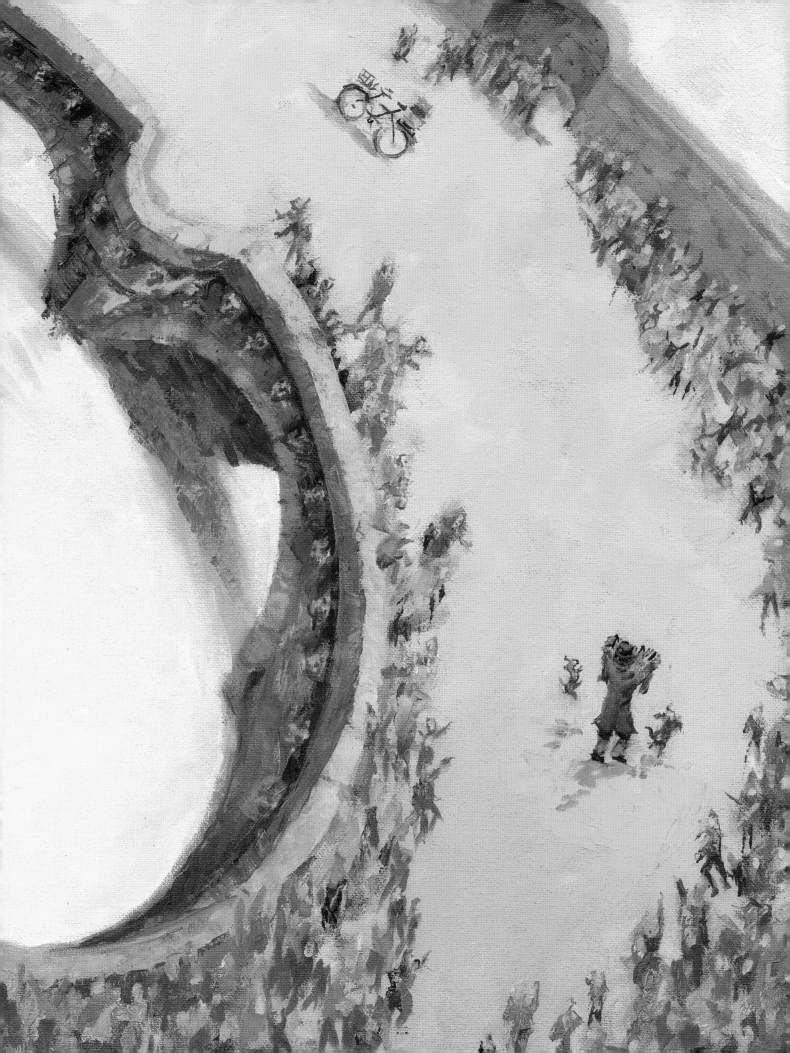